D0431944
WITHDRAWN

GREETINGS, SUN

by Phillis and David Gershator
paintings by Synthia Saint James

A RICHARD JACKSON BOOK
DK Publishing, Inc.

A Richard Jackson Book

DK Publishing, Inc.
95 Madison Avenue
New York, NY 10016
Visit us on the World Wide Web at http://www.dk.com

Library of Congress Cataloging-in-Publication Data
Gershator, Phillis.
Greetings, sun / by Phillis and David Gershator; illustrated by Synthia Saint James. —1st American ed.
p. cm.
Summary: Throughout the day, children greet the sun, the breeze, their breakfasts, their school, and all the other large and small sights which they encounter.
ISBN 0-7894-2482-7
[1. Day — Fiction. 2. Stories in rhyme.] I. Gershator, David.
II. Saint James, Synthia, ill. III. Title.
PZ8.3.G3235Gr 1997 [E]—dc21 97-34108 CIP AC

The text of this book is set in 18 point Joanna.
Printed and bound in the United States of America.
First Edition, 1998
2 4 6 8 10 9 7 5 3

Greetings, Dick.
A book's begun.
Greetings, Synthia.
Isn't it fun?
Greetings, Jennifer.
The book is done!
Greetings, greetings,
everyone.
—P.G. and D.G.

For Dr. Beverly J. Robinson
—S.S.J.

The stars are hiding,
all but one.
Good morning, good morning,
good morning, sun.

Greetings, sun.
Greetings, breeze.

Greetings, toes.
Greetings, knees.

Greetings, neck.
Greetings, nose.

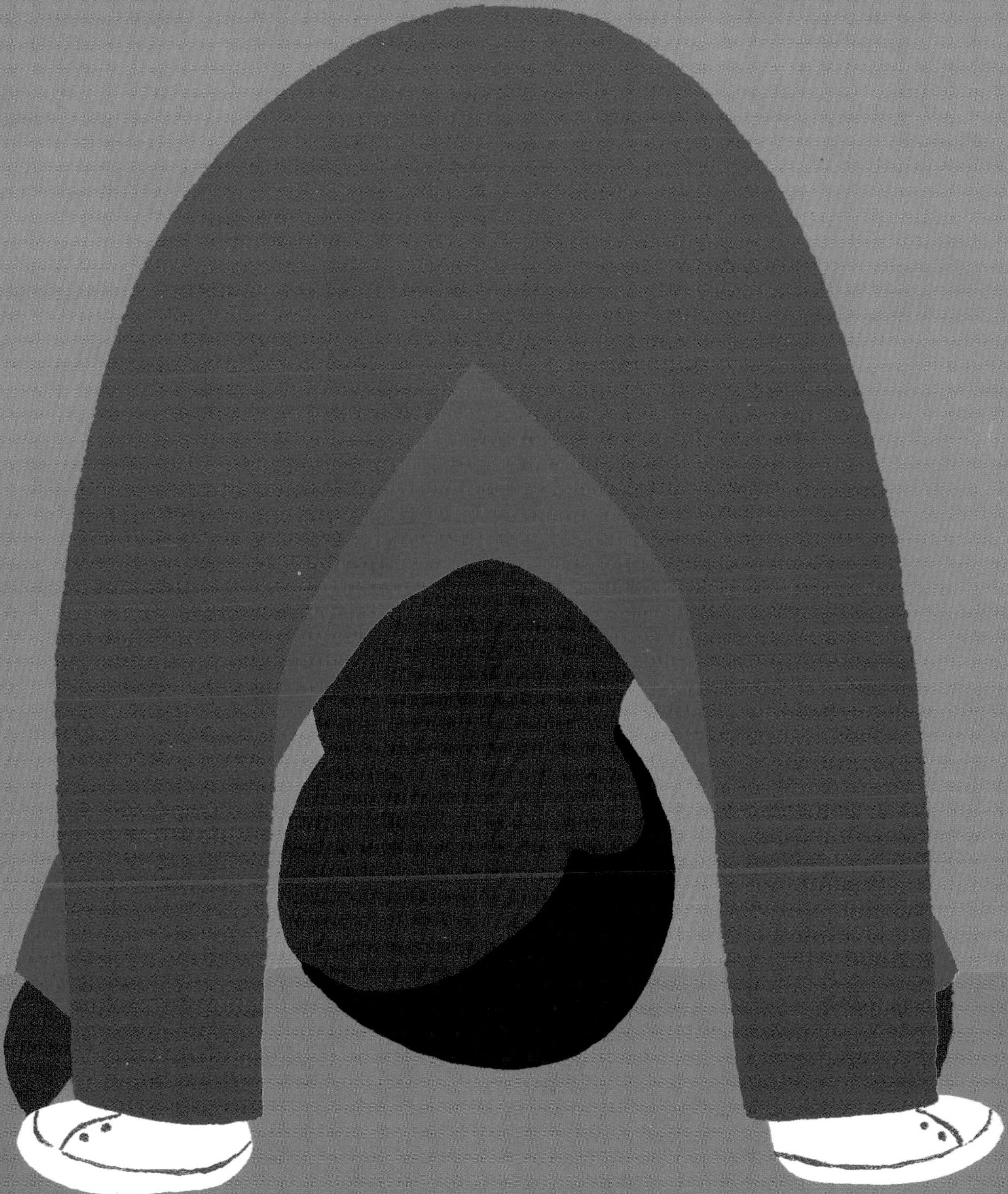

Greetings, shoes.
Greetings, clothes.

Greetings, toast.
Greetings, jelly.
Greetings, butter.
Greetings, belly.

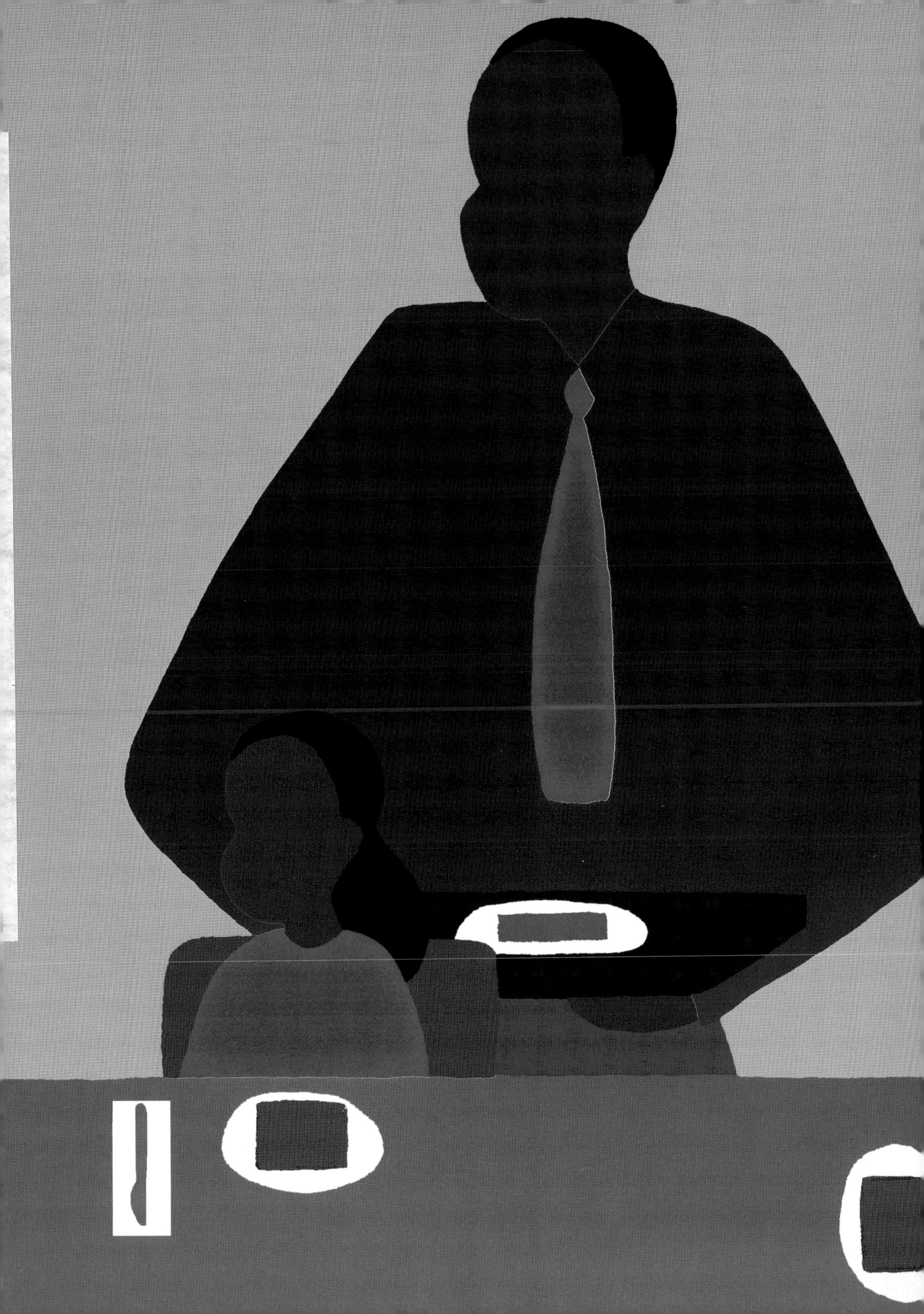

After breakfast out we go.
We hop. We jump. We shout "Hello!"

Greetings, sky.
Greetings, cloud.

Greetings soft.
Greetings loud.

Greetings, grass. Greetings, trees.

Greetings, ants.
Greetings, bees.

There's our school. It's not too far.
Greetings, school. Here we are.

Greetings, door.
Greetings, stair.

Greetings, rug.
Greetings, chair.

ABC

Greetings, girls.
Greetings, boys.
Greetings, books.
Greetings, toys.

Back at home, the end of day,
we sit in our seats and greet away.

Greetings, spoon. Greetings, plate.
Greetings early. Greetings late.

After dinner
it gets dark.

Birds sleep.
Dogs bark.

Greetings, pillow.
Greetings, bed.
Greetings, greetings
in my head.

The stars come out, all but one.
Good night, good night, good night, sun.

Greetings, moon.
And now we're done...

until it’s time to

greet the sun.